HUNGRY
Jim

By Laurel Snyder

Illustrated by
Chuck Groenink

chronicle books·san francisco

When Jim woke up on Tuesday,

his tail had fallen asleep.

This seemed odd.

Jim had never had a tail before.

From downstairs, Jim could hear his mother calling.

"Jim! Pancakes for breakfast!"

Jim's stomach began to growl.

She sounded DELICIOUS.

"I don't feel much like a pancake today," called Jim.

"Well, what *do* you feel like?" asked his mother.

Jim stared into the mirror.

He felt *beastly*.

Jim was not sure what to do.

On the one hand, he did *not* really want to devour his mother.

On the other hand . . .

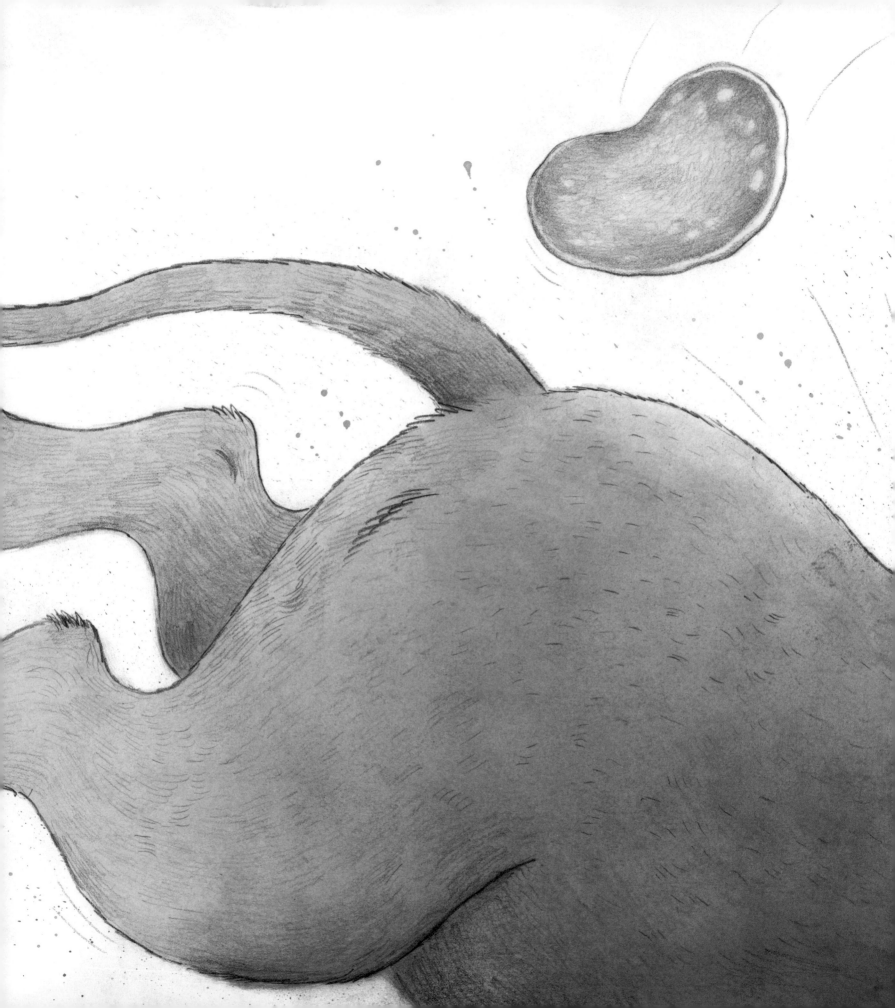

She *was* delicious.

Jim felt terrible.

But he was *still* hungry.

So Jim jumped out the window and ran away down the street.

There he met a dog.

And a dog-walker.

"This is awful," cried Jim as he ran.

"It's big. It's bad. It's truly the worst."

Jim's stomach only growled louder.

"Shut *up*," Jim told it. "Nobody asked *you*."

On Main Street, Jim met an old lady sweeping

and a girl with a donut.

The further he ran, the hungrier Jim became.

He wanted to eat anything.

He wanted to eat *everything*.

He wanted to cry.

Further down the road,

Jim came to a shop.

"*This* looks promising," he said.

And oh, it was!

"I hate you," Jim yelled at his stomach as he fled the scene.

Jim ran.

He ran some more.

He ran fast and away.

But wherever Jim ran, *there* he was.

At last, Jim came to a cliff.

He stood on the edge of the cliff.

The waves below him looked furious and confused.

"I know how you feel," said Jim.

Jim's stomach began to growl again.

"Shhh," said Jim. "Hush up. I'm trying to think."

Then Jim heard another growl.

It was the loudest growl yet.

"QUIET!" Jim said to his stomach.

But *this* growl was *not* coming from Jim's stomach.

It was coming from a bear.

The bear was tall and ugly.

The bear was full of teeth.

"Now I am going to EAT you," snarled the bear.

"Do you *have* to?" asked Jim.

"Pretty much," said the bear. "I'm a bear."

"Oh," said Jim.

But Jim's stomach disagreed.

It did not want to be eaten.

It gave a low growl of warning, and then, suddenly . . .

Jim was charging the bear.

He was springing and howling, pouncing and yowling.

He was loose and wild.

And oh, it felt GOOD!

"You're MINE, bear!" shouted Jim.

Then,

all at once,

Jim wasn't hungry anymore.

In fact, he was stuffed.

So he headed home.

Past the shop,

up Main Street,

and back down his own quiet block.

After a moment of deliberation,
Jim pounced back into the kitchen.

It was a huge relief to find things mostly as he'd left them.

But when he got to his room . . .

. . . Jim was faced with a dilemma.

Jim solved it.

He didn't feel even a little bit bad about that.

He only felt hungry.

For pancakes.

Chuck and Laurel humbly dedicate this book to the memory of the unrivaled Maurice Sendak, who is alive inside all of us, and occasionally peeks out in a book like this one.

We ate him up. We loved him so.

Library of Congress Cataloging-in-Publication Data:
Names: Snyder, Laurel, author. | Groenink, Chuck, illustrator.
Title: Hungry Jim / by Laurel Snyder ; illustrated by Chuck Groenink.
Description: San Francisco, California : Chronicle Books LLC, [2018] | ?2018
Summary: Jim wakes up hungry, just not for the pancakes his mother is
fixing—so his imagination takes over, and he pictures himself as a lion
checking out the possibilities for breakfast (including his mother).
Identifiers: LCCN 2015048857 | ISBN 9781452149875 (alk. paper)
Subjects: LCSH: Imagination—Juvenile fiction. | Appetite—Juvenile fiction.
Mothers and sons—Juvenile fiction. | CYAC: Imagination—Fiction.
Hunger—Fiction. | Mothers and sons—Fiction.
Classification: LCC PZ7.S6851764 Hu 2018 | DDC 813.6—dc23
LC record available at http://lccn.loc.gov/2015048857

Manufactured in China.

Typeset in News 701.
Design by Amelia Mack.

The illustrations in this book were rendered in pencil and Photoshop.

10 9 8 7 6 5 4 3 2

Chronicle Books LLC
680 Second Street
San Francisco, California 94107

Chronicle Books—we see things differently. Become part of our
community at www.chroniclekids.com.